CASE
FOR A
CREATOR
FOR KIDS

UPDATED AND
EXPANDED

Other books in the Lee Strobel series for kids

Case for Christ for Kids, Updated and Expanded

Case for Faith for Kids, Updated and Expanded

NEW YORK TIMES BESTSELLING AUTHOR

LEE STROBEL

WITH **ROB SUGGS** AND **ROBERT ELMER**

CASE
FOR A
CREATOR
FOR KIDS

UPDATED AND EXPANDED

ZONDER**kidz**

ZONDERVAN.com/
AUTHORTRACKER
follow your favorite authors

We want to hear from you. Please send your comments about this book to us in care of zreview@zondervan.com. Thank you.

ZONDERKIDZ

Case for a Creator for Kids, Updated and Expanded
Copyright © 2006, 2010 by Lee Strobel and Robert Elmer

Requests for information should be addressed to:

Zonderkidz, Grand Rapids, Michigan 49530

Library of Congress Cataloging-in-Publication Data

Strobel, Lee, 1952-
    Case for a Creator for kids / Lee Strobel with Rob Suggs and Robert Elmer. — Updated and expanded.
        p.   cm.
    ISBN 978-0-310-71992-2 (softcover)
        1. God — Proof, Teleological — Juvenile literature. 2. God — Proof, Cosmological — Juvenile literature. 3. God (Christianity — Juvenile literature. I. Suggs, Rob. II. Elmer, Robert. III. Title..
    BT107.S77 2010
    212'.1 — dc22   2009043681

Editor: Kathleen Kerr
Art direction: Kris Nelson
Cover design: Jody Langley
Interior design and composition: Luke Daab and Carlos Eluterio Estrada
Illustrations: © 2010 Terry Colon

Printed and bound in the UK using 100% Renewable Electricity at CPI Group (UK) Ltd

---

TABLE OF CONTENTS

Introduction:

WHO CAN YOU BELIEVE?

There you are sitting in science class at school. You're thinking ...

Say, what *are* you thinking? What are your feelings about science in general? Not as cool as a science-fiction movie? More fun than having a cavity drilled? Your true answer is in there somewhere.

Either way, it's science class. And it's an interesting one today, because Mr. Axiom, the science teacher, is starting a new unit on how the world began. You hear something about a Big Bang, and how all the stuff that made up the entire universe was gummed up into one puny little wad before it blew up. And how that stuff is *still* exploding outward, as it has since the beginning.

Fast-forward a couple of days. Now you're in Sunday school. Mrs. Homily, the teacher, is starting a new unit on the first book of the Bible, called Genesis. She starts with the very first words of Genesis, "In the beginning God created the heavens and the earth."

The kids are kind of nodding along, but you have a big question about all this. Why aren't Mrs. Homily and Mr. Axiom on the same page? They seem to have two completely different stories for the same subject. Mr. Axiom says the universe came from a big explosion; Mrs. Homily claims it came from God. Who's right and who's wrong?

What really bothers you the most is that Mr. Axiom, the science guy, seems to make the best case for his claims. A humongous, long-ago explosion seems like a pretty wild story, but he makes it believable. He gives numbers and details and tells why the scientists came up with their ideas.

You've always liked Mrs. Homily. What's weird is that she's only telling you what your parents might have told you all your life: God made everything. You've always liked church and gone along with the program. But you're not a little kid anymore. You're going to be a teenager soon. You're beginning to think things through for yourself. And you're noticing that neither Mrs. Homily nor anyone at church is too concerned about ... well, the *reasons* and the *evidence* for what they're teaching you. Not as much as in science class.

EVIDENCE:
proof that
something
happened

For example, you see a baseball lying in a pile of broken glass next to a window. That's your *evidence* that the baseball broke the window. Better hope that baseball isn't yours!

Question: What do you like or dislike about science? What kinds of science subjects have you enjoyed studying most?

Part 1
CASE FOR A CREATOR

Chapter 1
PIECING TOGETHER THE PUZZLE

So you've decided to assemble the whole puzzle for yourself. Who is right? Science or God? School or church? Both? Neither?

BEGINNING THE SEARCH

Get ready to do some detective work. You'll look for clues about how the world got here and whether God had anything to do with it — or whether there is a God in the first place.

But that's not so easy, is it? Since God is supposed to be invisible, and since he would have put this world together a long time ago, how will you get to the truth of the matter?

Well, it's all about detective work. Imagine you're looking for answers about some other question. Let's say ... well, pretend there's an elephant on your roof. One day you're leaving for school, and you see the massive animal sitting there on top of your house. Whoever put the elephant there is no longer on the scene. But your mom wants to know how that elephant got up there. (How to get him down would also be helpful information!) Where would you begin your investigation?

First, you might look for physical evidence. Are there footprints on the grass? A ramp or a ladder? Any cranes or elephant-moving equipment? You might take a walk all around the house and look closely for any changes. Whatever you find may tell you something about who might have put the elephant up there, and when it might have happened.

It might be a good idea to talk to some of the neighbors. Did they hear any strange noises? See any strange people? Maybe someone saw how the elephant was placed on the roof. It would also be a good idea to learn something about elephants. You might go to the zoo and talk to an elephant expert.

In other words, you would gather information by doing three things: looking, thinking, and asking. Finally, you would put together everything you learned and come to the best conclusion possible. Even if you couldn't absolutely prove the *who* and the *how* of the elephant caper, you might get enough information to make a very good guess.

CONCLUSION: an opinion decided based on facts. In the broken window example on the other page, your conclusion is realizing the baseball broke the window.

That's exactly how you would do your investigation of God. He himself may be invisible, but the evidence is not. You can look closely at several kinds of science. You can also talk to some really brainy scientists and experts who have already been collecting the clues.

- You can look very carefully.
- You can ask the best questions.
- You can think about what you learn.
- Then you can make the best decisions.

Question: Have you had to solve a mystery lately – such as a missing TV remote, for instance? How did you look, ask, think, and decide?

Any good scientist will tell you there is one important rule: follow the evidence wherever it leads you. For example, you might find trustworthy evidence that purple-polka-dotted aliens placed the elephant on the roof. That might be the best evidence you have. If so, your best guess would be that purple-polka-dotted aliens put an elephant on your roof — even if it sounds ridiculous, and even if people would laugh! Good science is *objective* — that means it looks only at the evidence, even if the evidence points to something we don't want to believe.

What if you want to believe in God? Look at the evidence, then make up your mind.

What if you want to believe there is no God? Same deal.

BEING OBJECTIVE:
to figure stuff out based on facts, not your own opinions

THREE BIG QUESTIONS

So what are the areas of science to think about? There are many to explore, but there are three important areas.

Your body is made up of cells. Cells are teeny-tiny things (you can't see them without a microscope) made up of even tinier things called proteins. Imagine a snowf lake. Millions and millions of snowflakes are packed together make a snowman – just like millions and millions of cells make you!

1. The first is called *cosmology*, which is the study of how the universe was formed. What can scientists tell us about the beginning of the world? And what can we conclude about whether God was involved or whether the universe came to be in some other way?

2. The next areas are *physics* and *astronomy*. Physics tells how things in the world work. For instance, if an elephant falls off your roof, it is because of gravity — and that's physics. If purple-polka-dotted aliens put the elephant there, they

might have come from outer space — and that deals with astronomy.

3. Then comes DNA and the question of human life. DNA is basically the instruction manual for building proteins, which make up the cells of all living things — including you. Is there any evidence that an intelligent designer put this complicated information into DNA? If not, where does the evidence lead?

After you examine these three big questions, you'll be in a better position to decide what you think about the biggest question of all — whether there is a case for a Creator. After that comes one final question: When the conclusion is made, what should you do about it? How should you live?

What you should do about it right now is turn the page!

Chapter 2
A BIG BANG BEGINNING

Okay, you've got to admit that an elephant on the roof is not something you see every day. You would have to immediately ask the question: how did it even get there?

But believe it or not, you see something much more amazing every day — and probably hardly give it a second thought. You see, there's a wide, wild, wonderful world around you. It's filled with blue oceans and skies, snowcapped mountains, and green valleys. All kinds of plants grow, and millions of animals creep, crawl, swim, and fly across it. The world has penguins and pandas, giraffes and gerbils, snakes and shrimp. And the planet spins in just the right way to give us and our animal friends bright days and dark nights.

It might be hard to get an elephant on your roof, but it would be tons more difficult to put all this stuff together and wrap it up in one planet — not to mention the galaxy and the universe where the world spins.

QUESTION: Does seeing the world every day make you take it for granted? Does seeing it every day make it any less incredible?

Sooner or later you have that thought: *Hey, this world is an amazing place, one blue-and-green marble out there among billions of miles of black space and barren rocks. How did our big marble get here?*

COSMOLOGIST:
a scientist who studies
the beginning of the
universe

There are scientists who spend all their time trying to figure out how the universe got started. *Cosmologists* are interested in that question. Just like a detective searching for clues to solve a mystery, you'll start by learning what *theories* or explanations the cosmologists have come up with.

THEORY:
an explanation
to answer a
question

THAT WAS A BLAST!

Most cosmologists believe it all started with a bang. And they mean exactly what they say.

MATTER: anything that has form and takes up room; the stuff everything is made of. Matter is all of the cells that make up this book, dirt, carpeting, toys, and even your body. If someone needs to drop a few pounds, they should say they need to lose matter instead of lose weight!

Here's how it happened, in cosmologists' view:

All matter — every last bit of all the stuff that *everything* (you, Earth, the sun — everything) is made of — was clumped together very, very, very tightly into a very, very, very small space. Before, it was nothing at all! Suddenly, it all exploded with a mighty blast. Imagine pushing everything you own into your bedroom closet, then forcing the door shut with all your strength. You'd better get out of the way! Pretty soon all that stuff will fly through the air of your bedroom. Multiply that by several bajillions of gazillions, and you would have the Big Bang.

Many scientists believe that when all those particles of matter exploded outward from the original wad of matter, they flew outward to fill the universe — and they're still moving, expanding the boundaries of the universe. Keep in mind that these particles were teeny tiny. The scientists call some of them *photons* — tiny particles that make light. So light filled the universe at the moment this explosion came.

PHOTONS: tiny particles of light

Horrendous Space Kablooie

In a famous cartoon strip, Calvin is a boy who talks to his imaginary tiger friend, Hobbes. Calvin wonders why something as amazing, mathematical, and scientific as the beginning of the universe would have a silly name like the Big Bang. Hobbes the tiger asks, "What would you call the creation of the universe?"

Calvin thinks for a moment and answers, "The Horrendous Space Kablooie!"

Many scientists began to use that name for the Big Bang, abbreviating it to the HSK!

The Big Bang, then, involved a great explosion of light. Hmmm. That seems familiar. It sounds just a bit like the first few sentences of the Bible, which say that in the beginning everything was "formless and empty" and then God said, "Let there be light."

Scientists have spent years trying to understand the Big Bang. They attempt to guess what happened then by studying what is happening now.

Question: Read the first four verses of the book of Genesis from the Bible. How would you compare these events to the Big Bang account of the beginning of the universe?

SOME OF THE SCIENTISTS' IDEAS

Idea #1: Pop start!

The first idea scientists offer is that sometimes matter "just shows up" for no reason. Some scientists say that the universe could have started this way. This idea says there would be no creator and no particular reason — it just happened because it could. Presto! Instant universe.

But that doesn't seem very scientific. Remember, science is what is observed in the way things happen. You know an elephant couldn't just appear out of nowhere on your roof. Someone or something had to put it there.

Idea #2: A universe that was caused

Our second idea is based on some thinking

by a Muslim who lived many centuries ago. It's called the Kalam Argument. Here's how it works:

Kalam Argument:

Everything that has a beginning has a cause.
The universe has a beginning.
So the universe has a cause.

Chapter 3

PUTTING KALAM TO THE TEST

$\mathcal{R}$ emember, the Kalam Argument is:

1. Everything that has a beginning has a cause.

2. The universe has a beginning.

3. So the universe has a cause.

1. Everything that has a beginning has a cause.

The Kalam Argument says that nothing new is created without being *caused*.

Try it at home! Your mom says something like, "Who made these muddy footprints on the carpet?" You shrug and say you don't know. Your brothers and sisters just look at one another innocently. What does your mother say? "Well, they didn't get there by themselves!"

The next time she says that, congratulate her for applying the Kalam Argument. Everything that has a beginning has a cause. The footprints began to exist at a point in time—so they *must* have had a cause!

This point makes sense. But a few scientists

VACUUM: completely empty space. It's not like the vacuum that sucks up dirt and dust at home. Say you attach a vacuum pump to a jar opening and suck out all the air so that nothing is left inside. Then seal the container before any air can get back in. What you'd have left inside is a vacuum—the kind you would find if you went to outer space. There's no air. No dirt. No dust. Nada.

are stubborn about their "pop start" theory. They speculate that the particles that make up the universe could have just popped out of nowhere from a certain kind of vacuum. A vacuum is usually defined as totally empty space. So who's right?

A professor named William Lane Craig has thought about this one for a long time. The vacuum

ENERGY: the ability to do work

that those scientists are talking about, he says, is not exactly "a big bunch of nothing" the way you imagined in the jar. This vacuum is full of energy. The vacuum and the energy locked up in the vacuum would have been the cause of those particles appearing – if that's what happened.

So that raises a very important question: who or what would have created this energy in the first place? Certainly its existence needs an explanation — and suddenly you're right back to the beginning of how the world got here! After all, this energy would seem to have needed a creator.

One thing seems like common sense: as far as human experience goes, nothing simply pops into existence on its own, out of nothing (that elephant on your roof can't appear out of nowhere). So the first step of the Kalam Argument holds up.

2. *The universe has a beginning*

When most scientists study all the facts and figures — and this can get pretty complicated — they become convinced that the universe had a beginning. And if there was truly a beginning, then there truly must be a cause. Just as the elephant on your roof didn't just pop into existence, the universe didn't create itself! There must be something — or someone — who caused the Big Bang to go kablooie!

Here is how the Bible explains where it started: "In the beginning God created the heavens and the earth." For thousands of years the Bible and its readers have insisted that there was a first moment when the universe came into existence. But only in the last hundred years or so have scientists discovered that all the clues really do point toward the universe having a beginning.

What about the proof? There are two kinds of evidence that the universe had a beginning: mathematical points and scientific points.

DOING THE MATH. Imagine you're going to a new movie on opening day. The line for tickets wraps around the edge of the mall and goes out of sight! If it's *infinite*, there would have to be people standing in that line as far back as you could check. In fact, there would be no beginning at all, just trillions upon trillions of people trying to get into the same movie theater. And they're in trouble, because there's only so much popcorn.

INFINITE OR INFINITY: no limits; an endless supply

Of course, there couldn't be an endless line of people. In the same way, the universe couldn't just stretch into the past forever, because the events could not go farther and farther into the past *forever*. By the way, another word for *forever* is *infinity* — an endless supply. The problem is that it's hard to talk about infinity because everything we can see and touch has limits.

Here's another example of the absurdity of an infinite number of things. Let's say you had an infinite number of baseball cards and you gave ten million of them to your friend. You'd still have as many cards as you did before you gave those away! Crazy, huh? Well, the idea that the universe is infinitely old is just as nonsensical.

DOING THE SCIENCE. The math people show us the numbers. The scientists show us the clues. And the clues from science, including measurements that researchers have done with high-tech instruments, point to our universe beginning with a bang. As a matter of fact, nearly all of today's scientists believe in the great explosion of light at the first moment of this universe's life.

So to review the first two Kalam points, everything that has a beginning has a cause, and the universe has a beginning. All you have to do is add up those two points to discover ...

3. The universe has a cause

Just as you would expect, something as big as the universe had to start somewhere. Think about it: you hear a "bang" from your bedroom, and your sister asks, "What was that?"

You reply from the living room, "Nothing." (Actually, you don't want her to know it's the stray elephant you sneaked into your bedroom, hoping to keep him for a pet.)

But your sister says, "That bang had to come from something." And of course, she's reminding you of the third part of the Kalam Argument. Now here's something to ponder: if a *little* bang had to have a cause, what about one as big as — well, everything all together?

What kind of cause could have started the entire universe? It must have been powerful, right? It must have been smart too, in order to make the explosion work just right. It must have been creative to come up with such a cool idea! It must

What's logic? It's kind of like common sense. Or to put it another way, logic is the study of the rules of reasoning. To have good arguments, you must obey the rules of logic or your argument isn't valid. The Kalam Argument obeys the rules of logic. If it's true that everything that begins to exist has a cause, and if it's true that the universe began to exist, then the rules of logic require the conclusion that the universe began to exist. That's logical, don't you think?

have been timeless, because time wasn't even created until the Big Bang happened. It must have been immaterial, or without a physical body. In other words, like a spirit.

Hmmm. Sound familiar? That's a pretty good start to describing God.

Could it be that Mr. Axiom, your science teacher, and Mrs. Homily, your Sunday school teacher, are *both* right? Details may differ, but they each agree that the universe was suddenly born in a flash of light at some point in the past. And logic tells you that the best explanation for all of this is a cause that looks suspiciously like the God of the Bible.

But who made God?

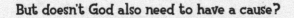

But doesn't God also need to have a cause?

No. Remember what you learned before – that everything with a beginning has to have a cause. Christians believe that God is eternal – he had no beginning and will have no end. In fact, before God created the universe, time didn't even exist. There was just timelessness.

So, since God didn't have a beginning he doesn't need a cause.

WANTED: DEAD OR ALIVE

Okay. So from the clues you read about, the universe points to a beginning. And it points to a *someone* who had to be there to start things up. But couldn't he have "left the building?" All you can say is that at some point, there *was* a God.

Science and mathematics point there, but no further. Right?

Not exactly. Consider these points:

- If someone is strong enough to create this whole universe, wouldn't he have to be strong enough to remain alive? Since he made the laws of nature, how could anything in them cause his death?

- You'll read later in the book how there is actually evidence that God is alive and well and still at work in his creation.

- Many scientists, like other people, say they get their clues about the Creator by knowing him as a friend. They point to many things that happen in their lives, and in the world, that show a Creator is alive and well.

Question: What do you think is the most sensible way to explain how the universe began? Why?

You still have a lot to read about! It's time to take a look at physics and astronomy.

Chapter 4
HITTING
THE COSMIC
LOTTERY

P lace: outer space.

You are an astronaut on the first flight to Mars.

Pretty cool, huh? Your hyper-powered ship plunges through space at warp speed, boldly hanging out where no kid has hung out before. You begin to get excited as your landing craft touches down on a dusty plain on Mars. You get into your space suit, climb down the ladder, and there it is: an attractively painted sign that reads, "Welcome to the Mars Holiday Inn Express."

Then you look past the sign and notice the escalator. It's a moving stairway that descends into an opening in the ground, just like at the mall. As you step aboard, it carries you to a nice underground complex made of swanky rooms — a restaurant with the aroma of burgers and pizzas coming from its kitchen, a bedroom to rest in after your trip, a rec room with exercise equipment, an indoor pool, and other nice stuff. It's just like a fine hotel back on earth. The only thing missing is — um, other beings, whether earthly types or otherwise.

The first thing to do is take a shower and wash off all that space grunge. Then, on the powerful radio next to your bed, you beam a message to earth. What to say? How about this?

Greetings from Mars! Arrived safely. Found interesting natural formations on the planet, probably formed by random weather conditions over millions of years. Lucky for me, the random rock and land formations grew into a natural hotel complex complete with working electricity, food, comfy furniture, and HBO. Hey, what were the odds?

What are odds? No, they're not a bunch of odd people. When someone asks, "What are the odds?" they're asking how likely it would be for something to happen. Let's say someone buys one lottery ticket. And let's say there's only one winning ticket out of a million tickets that were sold. Then your odds of buying that winning ticket would be one in a million. That's a long shot, don't you think?

What were the odds? Do you think random weather conditions would create a working escalator, an interplanetary radio, exercise equipment, and even a greeting sign? The odds of all that happening *by accident* would be one to some number far too large to even print out in a book this size (and that wouldn't be a very exciting book anyway).

Assuming you're halfway bright, you probably wouldn't send that message about "random weather conditions," would you? Of course not. More likely you would conclude that *someone had intentionally planned and built the interplanetary hotel complex.* Even though there's nobody around who might have done the job, that's still the most likely explanation.

Sure, it's a crazy story. But many scientists today would tell you that a swanky hotel on Mars — unplanned — is a lot like the idea of our complex universe without a builder.

COINCIDENCES?

Robin Collins is pretty smart. He went to college and got degrees in physics, mathematics, and philosophy. Sometimes people feel sort of dumb around him, but luckily he doesn't make a big deal out of how smart he is.

He says that in the past thirty years, scientists have learned a lot of new things about the universe and how it's all arranged. They have noticed that wherever they look, things are set up in *exactly, precisely* the right way for life to exist. In every direction, some *huge* coincidence would be needed for the conditions to all have just the

ANTHROPIC PRINCIPLE (AN-THRAH-PICK PRIN-SUH-PULL): the idea that the universe was created in exactly the right way to let human beings survive

right settings. And you would need a long string of these coincidences to occur *together*, side by side, at the same time, for life to be possible at all.

Many scientists agree with Dr. Collins. They make the point that the universe is exactly "fine-tuned" in such a way that it will support life. This is called the *anthropic principle*. That word *anthropic* comes from the Greek word for humanity. Think of one of those circus acrobats walking across a tightrope. She has fine-tuned her sense of balance to such an amazing degree that she can walk several hundred feet without tipping over to the right or to the left. The universe is like that, according to these scientists. Against far more amazing odds, it has found a precise balance in all its physical conditions, in just such a way that you can live in it.

But has it "arranged itself," or has some being of higher intelligence done the arranging? That is the great question, isn't it? That underground hotel back on Mars seems far more likely to have been arranged by a "someone" than by random environmental conditions. And in the case of the tightrope, a baby couldn't crawl across the wire. It took a special athlete working very hard to *purposely* fine-tune the right balance.

In the same way, many scientists find it highly unlikely that random conditions in the universe would fall into line in just such a way that we would have a nice home — unless someone intentionally fine-tuned the right balance.

Question: What is one coincidence you have seen happen? How likely or unlikely was it?

GRAVITY: THE TALE OF THE TAPE

There's a bumper sticker that reads, "Gravity: It's not just a good idea — it's the LAW!"

The law of gravity is an example of a kind of physics we can easily understand. The earth pulls at everything that is either on it or close to it. It pulls at you, and that's why you don't float off into the sky. It pulls at the moon, and that's why the moon follows our planet everywhere. The moon doesn't just figure it's a good idea to follow the earth; it's the *law*.

LAW OF GRAVITY: attraction between two objects. If you were to jump out of an airplane, you would eventually hit the ground (hopefully you have a parachute!).

Gravity has a certain amount of strength. It could have been much weaker or much stronger, but it's set at a certain level. In fact, imagine a tape measure that stretches all the way across the universe — billions and billions of miles. Pretend it has marks at every inch. This represents the range along which gravity could have been set. However, it's set at one precise mark along that long tape measure — and because it's exactly where it needs to be, life is possible.

Now imagine we changed the setting by moving it just *one inch* on the tape measure. That's one inch compared to the width of the entire universe. Doesn't seem like much of an adjustment, does it? Actually, that small change could create a universe-wide catastrophe. Life would be destroyed everywhere. But because gravity is fixed at precisely the right location, life is possible. (Good thing, right?)

> If you were to land on Jupiter and try to walk out of your spaceship, you'd be as flat as a pancake against the ground because the level of gravity is so strong.

Could that be just a coincidence? Something that worked out just right on its own?

It's like hitting the cosmic lottery, isn't it? As you read earlier, when somebody wins the lottery, his or her chances may have been a million to one or several million to one. But the chances of the universe having worked out just right on its own are much, much smaller — again, one chance in a number with so many zeros behind it you could not even print them out.

A scientist speaks

"A commonsense and satisfying interpretation of our world suggests the designing hand of a super-intelligence." – Owen Gingerich, Harvard astronomy professor and senior astronomer at the Smithsonian Astrophysical Observatory

A ROOM FULL OF MONKEYS

If gravity were the only condition required for life, we would be impressed at how perfectly our universe sets it up for us. But there are many other factors involved in making it possible for you to live, breathe, and exist. There are at least thirty separate necessities for living, and each one of them is finely tuned to allow you to exist.

> Some necessities for living are food, water, and air. Gravity is one of them. Without gravity, you would float to outer space. By the way, so would your food, water, and air!

There is an old saying that claims if you had a room full of monkeys and gave each one a computer with a keyboard, sooner or later one of them would produce a duplicate of one of Shakespeare's plays, like *Romeo and Juliet*. (Wouldn't you hate the job of checking their work?) It's not that one of the monkeys would become a great creative writer — just that he would hit all the right keys by chance. The question is, how many bajillions of years would it take for that to happen?

The universe is like that, only it's much more complicated than a single play by Shakespeare.

We have an orderly place that allows a variety of life-forms — a possibility that is so, so, so fragile. Is it easier to explain by coincidence, like monkeys tapping away at the keyboard? Or is it easier to explain as a personal, intentional work of superintelligence and creativity? The theory of *intelligent design* covers the second choice.

Another example of "fine-tuning" is the *cosmological constant*. Pretty fancy name, huh? So what does it mean? It's the energy density of empty space. So what does *that* mean?

Well, here's what you need to know about the cosmological constant: it had to be set absolutely perfectly, or a terrible disaster would have resulted. If it had been adjusted just slightly in one direction, stars and planets could never have formed. If it had been changed just slightly in the other direction, the whole universe would have collapsed upon itself. Instead, the cosmological constant is one exact mark on the tape measure — the only mark that will allow life to exist in the universe.

INTELLIGENT DESIGN: the belief that the order of our universe and its living things shows evidence of a thinking designer rather than coincidence

How precise is the cosmological constant? "Let's say you were way out in space and were going to throw a dart at random toward the earth," Dr. Robin Collins said. "It would be like successfully hitting a bull's-eye that's one-trillionth of a trillionth of an inch in diameter. That's less than the size of one solitary atom."

Now, take the two measurements you've learned: gravity and the cosmological constant. Getting the precise setting of either one alone is more amazing than you can imagine. But the two *together*? According to Dr. Collins, the chances of that are about one part in a hundred million trillion trillion trillion trillion trillion trillion. Try counting to that number sometime when you can't sleep!

Now consider that there are many other measurements found in physics. Imagine a giant dashboard, like the one in a car, with all those readings. You can believe either that they have set themselves on their own, or that someone has sat in the driver's seat and carefully set them at the right readings. Intelligent design says there must be a driver.

Question: As you look at all the factors making life possible in our universe, do you believe it's likely that there are other planets with life? Why or why not?

DESIGNING MINDS

Dr. Collins makes an interesting point. He says that the more he studies the universe, the more amazed he is.

"Only recently have we discovered how precise every condition had to be, in so many areas, for us to have this universe that allows life," he said. "The deeper we dig, we see that God is more subtle and more ingenious and more creative than we ever thought possible. And I think that's the way God created the universe for us — to be full of surprises."

So what's your take? Did you start with a big bang and end up — just by chance — with thinking people who live in a wonderful world of grassy fields, oceans, blue skies, and four seasons? If so, we won the lottery of all lotteries. There could have been a massive universe made up only of flying rocks, and created by no one in particular for no purpose in particular.

But look around you! It's not too hard to agree with more and more scientists who look away from their telescopes and microscopes and say, "Somebody up there likes us!"

And you haven't even read about DNA yet!

Chapter 5

MOUSETRAPS AND ASSEMBLY INSTRUCTIONS

There's a board game called Mousetrap. It's all about building a "machine" that is much more complicated than it needs to be — and much more fun! There's a bathtub on top of a pole, a little man who launches off a springboard, a little silver ball that rolls down a chute, a stick with a boot at the end that kicks the ball down that chute when something nudges it, and lots of other junkyard treasures. In the game, you assemble the trap by adding each crazy piece.

It may be the most enjoyable mousetrap you can build, but it certainly isn't the simplest. You can find the simpler kind at your local hardware store — or at the office of Michael Behe, a respected biochemist. He is the type of scientist who studies what living things are made of, especially what the chemicals are up to inside them. And he loves playing with one of those simple mousetraps made of a rectangle of wood. You have to worry about his fingers. But he shows you each of the parts — the base, the catch, the spring, the holding bar, and the hammer — and how they work together.

Then you go, "Wait a minute! I thought you were into chemicals and cells and stuff."

And he goes, "I am. Now — which of these parts can I take away from the mousetrap and keep it working?"

And you go, "I don't know. Looks like you need 'em all."

And he goes, "Right! So the mousetrap is an example of *irreducible complexity*. That means it is a machine that cannot be simplified any further and still do its job. Take away the hammer here, for instance, and how many mice could you still catch? One-third? One-half?"

"None? Hey! Watch your fingers!"

"Right again!" Then he stuffs the mousetrap back into a drawer. He says, "The cell is run
by irreducibly complex micromachines."

IRREDUCIBLE COMPLEXITY:
the simplest possible arrangement
of a machine for doing a job

That's right — there are microscopic motors
and systems in living organisms — including you!
In a way, they're like the mousetrap because a
certain number of their parts must be in place
for the machine or system to work.

For example, some bacteria have a teeny, tiny
motor and a rotary propeller to help them move
through liquids — a motor so advanced that it
spins faster than the engine on those fancy sports
cars you see on the covers of car magazines. A
professor at Harvard University says it's the most
efficient motor in the universe, but it's so small
your eye can't even see it — no matter how hard
you squint!

Here's the point: It's impossible for the parts of this microscopic motor to have suddenly come together on their own, and there's no known way they could have been pieced together by themselves over time. So that leaves one other explanation: that there's a designer behind them.

"If the creation of a simple device like a mousetrap requires Intelligent Design," said Dr. Behe, "then we have to ask, 'What about the finely tuned machines of the cellular world?'"

If there's no natural way these machines could have been built on their own, he said, then other explanations should be considered.

After years of research and study, Dr. Behe has reached his own conclusion. "I believe," he said, "that irreducibly complex systems are strong evidence of a purposeful, intentional design by an intelligent agent. No other theory succeeds."

BIOCHEMISTRY: the study of stuff found in living things and of the chemical activities that take place in living things.

Could that "intelligent agent" be the same one who wrote the assembly instructions for all the parts of your body? Wait a minute! Who said anything about assembly instructions?

ASSEMBLY INSTRUCTIONS AND BIOLOGY

Have you ever put together something that's pretty complicated, like a model airplane that started out as a box full of seemingly unrelated pieces? What guided you to put the right parts together — this little widget attaching to this gizmo, this tab inserting into that slot? That's right — grab the instructions! Without them, the chances of building an airplane on your own would be really slim.

Now think about a *real* airplane, like a giant airliner that carries hundreds of people. Millions of parts have to be fit together in precisely the right way in order to build an airplane that seems to defy gravity as it soars through the sky. Without assembly instructions, it would be impossible to guess how to put together a safe and working airplane.

Think about this: you are much more complex than any airplane. Human beings can build airplanes, but they can't build a human being like you. How did the trillions of cells that make up your body get put together exactly so? Right again — assembly instructions!

Your body is composed of one hundred trillion microscopic cells. If you were to crack open any one of those cells, you'd find a long, thread-

DNA: the "instruction manual" for building each life-form

like material coiled up inside. Stretch it out, and it would measure six feet long! On that thread would actually be a chemical alphabet containing the exact assembly instructions for all of the proteins to make your skin, organs, hands, eyes, and brain. It's kind of like a super-duper complex recipe!

These assembly instructions are called DNA, which stands for **D**eoxyribo**N**ucleic **A**cid. Long, threadlike structures known as chromosomes carry genes with their DNA information. These genes are passed on from parent to child. If you share your mother's blue eyes or your father's running speed, it is because the right genes were passed to you from that parent.

After many years of work, scientists finally mapped out the *billions* of codes that make up the entire set of human chromosomes. It was like the complete assembly instructions for putting together people like you. But who could have devised those billions of codes in the first place?

No, your parents didn't pass their blue jeans down to you. Have you ever noticed that sometimes kids might laugh exactly like one of their parents? Or be really good at a hobby like basketball, just like one of their parents? That's because kids received the same genes from the parent.

SCRAMBLED LETTER GAME

Now it's time to think about spelling. Have you ever noticed how one misplaced letter can change the whole meaning of a word, then a sentence? You might tell someone, "I caught your act."

But if you reversed two letters, you could have, "I caught your cat." There are twenty-six letters in the alphabet, and they can be scrambled and re-scrambled to make any word in the language. Language is like a careful game of Scrabble.

Think of DNA as an alphabet that conveys information. Instead of twenty-six letters, DNA has only four letters that represent chemicals. Scientists use the letters *A*, *C*, *G*, and *T*. These letters spell out the exact way your body can put together the complicated proteins that make up your body. In fact, your body has thousands of different kinds of proteins that create your fingers and toes, teeth and eyes, ears and brain, and all of the organs, tissues, blood, and nerves inside you.

Bill Gates, president of Microsoft, has said that DNA is like a software program, but far more complex than any software program that has ever been written. Your computer is useful for homework, e-mail, surfing the Internet, and playing computer games. But many, many software experts have labored for years to produce the codes that make that possible.

Do you think the far more complicated codes that provide the assembly instructions for every single person on earth — and every single human being who has ever lived — could be "written" without there being a software engineer of life?

Imagine opening a box of Scrabble tiles, shaking it up really well, and throwing all the tiles into the air. How would they land? If you were extremely fortunate, you might find that three or four letters have landed in such a way as to make a short word. The rest would be gibberish. But can you imagine throwing the letters into the air time after time and having them land in such a way that sentences, paragraphs, and whole books landed in order right in front of you? Seems awfully unlikely — unless some invisible intelligence had control over how those letters landed.

To sum it up: You live in the age of information. Think of all the information

1. *on websites,*
2. *in e-mails,*
3. *that bounces off satellites and makes a cable television program in your living room,*
4. *in all the books in all the libraries in the world.*

Every bit of *that* information is put together by human beings. You can't receive an e-mail that wasn't written by a human being, see a television show that wasn't created by people, or read a book that had no human author.

Scientists discover more and more that life itself is made up of *information*, like the assembly instructions of DNA. That information is far more complicated and meaningful and exact than all the books and e-mails and television broadcasts in the world. Could it all come together to form the human population of earth just by "letter tiles" falling on a great biological playing board?

Wherever you see information of any kind, there was an intelligence behind it. Since there's information coded inside the DNA of every living person and thing, doesn't that mean life has an author? A designer with an intelligence far too great for anyone to understand?

Many scientists today believe that every cell in your body bears the signature of that designer in the DNA that's found there — and that he is very much alive, very well, and still producing masterpieces every day.

Question: Who is the designer of DNA?

Chapter 6

IS THIS YOUR FINAL ANSWER?

At the beginning of this book, you learned about true science: following the facts no matter where they lead.

It's like putting together a big jigsaw puzzle, isn't it? In the beginning you have a great number of pieces with many combinations of colors and pieces of pictures. None of them alone tell the story. But as you put the puzzle together, a greater picture begins to assemble before your eyes. Your only job is to keep finding where the pieces go. When they're all in place, the picture is very clear.

How do you feel about the puzzle you put together in this book? Each chapter is a piece of the puzzle.

- Cosmology is the study of the origin of the universe. Everything that has a beginning has a cause behind it. Most scientists now believe the universe had a beginning at some point in the past. That means there must be a cause behind it — a powerful, smart, creative, timeless, and immaterial cause, like a spirit. In fact, like God.

- Physics is the study of energy and motion, and astronomy is the study of outer space. The conditions that make life possible in the universe are so specific, and so completely necessary, that it's hard to imagine anything more unlikely than for them to fall into place on their own. For example, if there was a teeny-tiny bit more gravity strength or a teeny-tiny bit less, the effect on life would be a disaster. Hmmm. Sounds like whoever created the universe must have really cared about people because he was so careful to create a safe and livable place for them.

• DNA contains the instructions for creating the human body, and biochemistry is the study of chemical activities that take place in living things. Your entire body is a fantastic complex — a whole world, really — of factories filled with micromachines that churn out all the work that makes it possible for you to eat, breathe, and do everything else. Living things contain microscopic machines that can't be explained by saying they somehow put themselves together. A more reasonable explanation is that there's a creator behind them. In fact, the assembly instructions for all living things are made up of information found in DNA. And wherever information is — whether in a book or a computer code — there's intelligence behind it. In the case of DNA, it's a superintelligence — something like God.

You may be thinking, *What to decide?*

WHAT THE SCIENTISTS THINK

Some scientists decide there's no Creator. They look at the universe outside us and conclude it must have somehow been created without any help. They look at the vast complexity of living things and conclude that it's all a matter of cells that combined together over time through chance, until they somehow found their way toward becoming more complex life-forms. They believe God isn't needed in any of this, so he must be an idea made up by people.

Other scientists decide that there *must* be a Creator. They say the universe and living things show too much order to believe otherwise. The combination of all the cells and all the chemicals and all the laws of physics would call for coincidences beyond any mathematical calculation — just to allow us to live. They look at the beauty of the earth, set in a cold and empty space. The four seasons. Wind and rain and everything you need — not only to live but also to enjoy life. They look at all these things and wonder how anyone could think that there is no intelligent being behind it all.

A brilliant surgeon named Viggo Olsen once believed there was no God. His wife shared his lack of belief. But the two of them finally decided to search out all the evidence, as you have started to do by reading this book. They were going to show once and for all how science disproved God.

They began by attempting to list all the scientific errors in the Bible.

To their great shock, they couldn't find those mistakes. When they checked out each supposed "error," they found out it wasn't a mistake after all. They had simply not understood what the Bible actually said.

As they looked at each area of science, they failed again and again to disprove God. Instead, they kept finding huge reasons to believe in God after all. Not only that, but they came to believe that science pointed to several specific truths about God:

- The universe was created, and it's packed with power — heat and energy, for instance. Therefore, it was created by a *mighty force*.

- They looked at the order in the universe and in the cell structure of human bodies and decided that this creator must be *intelligent*.

- They looked at the ability of people to love and to have compassion and concluded that we must have been created by someone with those same qualities.

Their conclusion was that there is a God

who is very powerful, very intelligent, and very caring. And after they investigated history, as you can do if you read *Case for Christ*, they were finally led to believe that Jesus Christ is God's Son, sent into this world to personally befriend the very people God created.

The Olsens set out to show there was no God, and particularly that Christianity was a myth. Instead, they found themselves wanting to know Jesus. They asked him to send them to the place where they could serve him best of all. They ended up in the suffering nation of Bangladesh, where they spent thirty-three years, worked to start 120 churches, and helped provide doctors and medicine for countless hungry and sick men, women, and children. They said this was the most wonderful and exciting and fulfilling adventure of their lives.

After working with Jesus among the poor, they were more convinced than ever that God is powerful, intelligent, and very loving.

FACTS AND FAITH

Like other scientists, the Olsens discovered that the greatest evidence of God is very personal. As interesting and informative as all the fields of

science may be, their own experience was the final and most powerful item of evidence.

Many scientists believe in God not only because of what they see in microscopes and telescopes, but what they experience in *relationship*. They feel that God isn't just some cosmic force out there on the other side of their calculations and chemicals. They feel that he is someone right here living in their daily lives. In other words, faith begins where facts leave off.

So as the investigation comes to a close, it's time to decide what to do about it.

What do you think about God? Do you believe science points in his direction? If so, what do you think he is like?

And if you believe there is a God, what difference does that make in your life? Should you just say, "Oh, that's interesting!" and go on the way you were? Or should you live in a new way?

Would you agree that if there is a God, he went through a lot of trouble to leave all kinds of clues to his existence in cosmology, astronomy, physics, biochemistry, and DNA? Why would he do that? Because he wants you to find him!

And would you agree that if he is very mighty and very caring, as the Olsens decided, that he might be a wonderful friend for you?

If so, what's your final answer? That is, how do you respond to what you have decided?

People all over the world have found faith to match their facts. They love God, they enjoy his friendship, and they find great happiness in serving him every day.

If you're interested in that kind of life, you might try an experiment. Try that faith out. Ask God to speak to your heart. Ask him to come into your life, just as a good friend would come into your home. See what happens. And as part of your experiment, talk to your parents about God.

Also, try doing something that you think God would want you to do, just as the Olsens did. You don't have to go to another country. Just try doing something nice for another person — someone in your family or at school. This is an important part of your experiment because God-believers say that doing what God likes helps us know God better.

As you grow each day, becoming older and smarter, keep experimenting! Continue to know God more and more. It's the greatest science project of all.

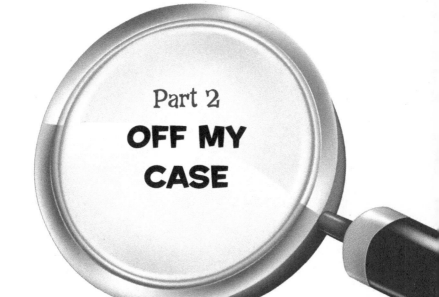

Part 2

OFF MY CASE

Sometimes there's a pretty wide gap between Sunday school lessons and real life, isn't there? On one hand, it's not hard to understand a Bible verse like 1 Peter 3:15: "Always be ready to give an answer to anyone who asks you about the hope you have." But ...

Are you ready?

Well ... maybe. But it's okay to admit that we sometimes let a chance to share our faith slip by. After all, for most of us it's hard to think of just walking up to someone and telling them how much Jesus loves them — even if we know it's true!

So that's why we're including this section of the book: some stories to help you see that everyday life is full of open doors to present the case for a creator.

You'll read four short stories of everyday kids in everyday situations. Well, mostly everyday situations. Maybe you've never ridden in a 3-G space simulator before. But no matter what, you'll be able to relate to the kids and the everyday jams they get themselves into.

Oh, and if any of the stories ring a bell in other ways, that's because they're built on ideas you've already learned by reading this book.

In other words, these stories explain many of the cool ways to help us better understand Bible truths. Things like "Can I really be a Christian if I have some doubts?" These stories start with those kinds of questions, but then shows us what might happen if kids draw pictures of the truth using their lives as pencils and paper.

Of course, they're not all perfect kids, and sometimes they mess up. But hey, what else is new?

As you read, imagine yourself in each of the stories. That way, you'll start seeing how everyday stuff in your own life can open the door to faith in exciting new ways. Let the stories give you ideas of your own. More important, take a couple of minutes at the end of each story to answer the Go Ahead, Stump Me! questions. Don't worry! You won't be graded, and we didn't write them to give you a hard time. But we guarantee they'll help you start thinking about how to work these ideas into your own life. After all, that's what *Case for a Creator* is all about.

So have fun with the stories, and as you read them you'll discover brand-new ways to make a case for a creator. And see? It's not that hard after all!

Chapter 7

HAPPY FOURTHDAY TO YOU

Brandon chuckled as he stuffed another "China Dragon" firecracker into the can. Safe and sane fireworks? These church kids needed somebody to show them how to have a little fun. So while nobody was looking he'd just introduce them to the "Brandon Rogers Special," and boy, were they going to be surprised!

"Surprise!" Everyone at the picnic cheered when Shawn's mother brought out the cake — red, white, and blue, with twelve candles shaped like firecrackers. Of course, no one was surprised. But Shawn didn't mind that he was born on the Fourth of July. The good part was that the whole family usually showed up for the traditional party at Hoover Lake Park. People from church sometimes came. Plus, he could invite whichever friends he wanted. Only this year was going to be different.

"Be sure to let your friend have a big piece." Mom was always thinking of the guests. And Brandon, the new kid at St. Michael's Christian School, didn't seem to mind — even though he'd already eaten about four hot dogs and half a watermelon all by himself. The guy was a bottomless pit.

"So, Brandon," Shawn's mother asked as she cut more cake, "how did you like St. Michael's? I know you were only there for the last two months, but — "

"It was fine," he answered, loading up with another big mouthful of cake. End of discussion. Of course, there were all kinds of kids at Shawn's school. Lots of Christians, and lots of, well ... kids like Brandon.

"So when are the fireworks?" he asked be-tween mouthfuls of cake.

"You mean the big bang?" Shawn looked at his watch, glad they were changing the subject, wondering where the other kids had disappeared to. "As soon as it gets dark. Twenty minutes, maybe. Only it's not such a big deal. We just light off some red, white, and blue sparkler things and push them out in a raft. It's pretty cool out there on the water, but I don't really know why we call it the big bang."

"Yeah, well, back home in Houston, we used to have a really awesome neighborhood party on the Fourth. We launched, like, tons of rockets, firecrackers, the works. The big ones were like a hundred dollars a pop."

"My dad would never let us do that." Shawn chuckled and looked at their modest little fire-works stash down by the beach. Dad had always been pretty strict about staying safe, who got to light the sparklers, all that. While they were wait-ing, though, he thought he'd better ask Brandon more about himself. Make him feel comfortable.

"So do you miss your friends from Houston? Your old school, that kind of thing?"

"School? You've got to be kidding!" Brandon looked around for a second piece of cake. "I only had one good teacher there. That was Mr. Jacobs, my science teacher. He was really cool."

"Yeah?" Shawn waited for his new friend to explain.

"He was really into creation of the universe stuff. We all had to do a report on the big bang."

"Cool! So did we!" Finally something they had in common, maybe. They started down the little grassy hill toward the beach. "We got to write how we think God created the universe in one big explosion, where everything basically started out in one place, and how lots of scientists are starting to see that the creation stuff in the Bible makes a lot of sense, and — "

But he didn't finish, with Brandon laughing so hard. What was so funny?

"It's not you." Brandon wiped his eye with the sleeve of his shirt. "It's just that the only time Mr. Jacobs ever mentioned God was one time when I heard him in the parking lot, after he shut the door on his thumb. He's not like any of our teachers at St. Michael's."

"Maybe not, but ..." Shawn tossed another stone. Why not ask? Brandon had left the door open. "But what about you?"

"Me?" Brandon took his time choosing a smooth stone to skip, then wound up and let loose.

"If I told you, you'd kick me out of your Christian birthday party."

"Oh, come on. Really."

Another pause, another stone skipped out across the glassy lake.

"All right, well ... I think the big bang idea is cool and everything. Whatever works for you. But I think Mr. Jacobs might have been right. I just don't think God made it happen."

"Huh?" Shawn didn't get it. "Then who did?"

"Nobody."

"You're kidding."

Brandon shook his head. Wow. Shawn might have guessed that's what Brandon thought, but it was still weird to have someone come right out and say so.

"I mean, no offense or anything, but ..." Brandon turned back toward the food table, and again the conversation was over. Well, okay. By then it was time to get the big bang going anyway, if Shawn could find his dad. So he ran up to the horseshoe pits and over to the swing sets, but it was getting too dark to tell. Finally he decided his dad might have already headed down to the beach, so a few minutes later he hurried down the path and through the bushes.

"Shawn, wait! Don't go out — "

Shawn heard the voice behind him just as he stepped out onto the gravel beach, just as the flash of light blinded him, like lightning.

And then he remembered falling over backward, and nothing more until he woke up on the grass, surrounded by people.

"He's waking up," said Shawn's dad. Oh, so there he was. "Everybody, give him some breathing room."

Well, that was fine, but what he really needed was an aspirin.

"Whoa, my head." He felt his forehead, where someone had stuck a large bandage. His temples throbbed. "What ... was I struck by lightning?"

Not likely, but that's what it felt like. Some birthday!

"It's all my fault." Brandon knelt next to him, and it sounded like he was crying. "I tried to stop you from going down there after I lit the fuse, but ..."

Shawn wasn't quite sure what he'd just heard.

"You lit a fuse? What fuse?"

"I put some firecrackers in a can, and I think a piece of metal might have hit you in the forehead. It was really stupid of me. But I didn't think ..."

"It's okay." Shawn rubbed his forehead, glad he was still in one piece.

But that didn't stop Brandon from saying he was sorry, again and again, in the car and all the way to the emergency room for stitches.

"Really, it's okay." Shawn finally held up his hand as they were sitting in the emergency waiting room, hanging around until Shawn's name was called. Brandon let out his breath, like he'd been holding it the whole time.

"That was sure a big bang, though, huh?"

"Yeah." Shawn did his best to smile. "Only I guess this one didn't just happen by itself, either."

Well, maybe Brandon didn't see it Shawn's way — yet. And Shawn could think of much less painful ways to prove his point about big bangs.

Briefcase

- Fireworks set off fires that caused $35 million in damage a few years ago, according to the U.S. Fire Administration. During that same time, 9,300 people were hurt, many of them seriously. Almost half were under age fifteen.

- Most astronomers and scientists today believe in some kind of big bang theory, in which the universe is said to have started in a giant fireball of light. Most don't tend to believe that God is responsible for the creation of the universe, though.

Go Ahead, Stump Me!

- What is the big bang theory? How do you think the universe was created?

- What would you say if someone disagreed with you about how the world was created?

- Read the first chapter of Genesis in your Bible. Do you see anything about a big bang or anything like it? Do you think scientists might be right about big bangs and wrong about other things?

Chapter 8
TAKE ME OUT TO THE DERBY

BAM!

Izzy winced and plugged her ears as the big blue car streaked out of nowhere and smacked into the passenger side of the old white station wagon. She peeked over at her older cousin Alex, who was grinning at her.

"What's the matter, Izzy?" He poked her with his elbow. "Don't ya'll have demolition derbies back home in Chicago?"

"Yeah, we do." She had to shout above the roar of the crowd and the crash-roar of the derby. "We call them *rush hour*."

Well, that got a laugh. But it didn't get Izzy out of the mess she was in: having to sit through the loudest grandstand show in history with her older cousin, her parents, Aunt Nancy, and Uncle John. Watching twenty-five clunker cars in the middle of a dirt football field, crashing into one another until just one was left running. She checked her watch again.

Smash! Another hit. Another cheer. Well, obviously people liked this kind of thing, so Izzy didn't want to be rude. After all, she saw this part of her family only once every summer, when she and her parents visited Atlanta. And she had promised to be sociable. Coming along to the demolition derby was sociable.

She'd also promised to keep praying for Alex and his family. Be a witness.

"If we're not," her mom had asked her weeks ago, "who will be?"

Right. But that was before her cousin had come back home from college with all the answers. Like how obvious it was that humans evolved from monkeys.

Huh? Half the time Izzy had no idea what he

was talking about — except that it didn't sound at all like what she'd read in her Bible. Still, she felt like she had to be polite and nod, even when Alex kept showing off all his crazy new ideas.

CRUNCH!

Izzy jumped off the bench, which made Alex laugh all over again.

"Chill out." He pointed at a cloud of smoke. "Look, it's over, see? Number fifty-seven won."

Terrific. The driver of a purple-and-gray wreck waved at the cheering crowd as he circled the other dead and crunched cars.

"Survival of the fittest, huh?" Alex put on that smirk that signaled he was about to pass out a little more college wisdom. "Just one more example of how evolution works."

"You're kidding, right?" This was too lame. He actually believed that smashed cars at the demolition derby proved ... what?

"No, look." Alex pointed to a big green car with the back end curled up. "See that Chevy there?"

The one with all the smoke coming out of it? He went on.

"That's a '79. You can tell by the front end."

What was left of it. But Professor Alex wasn't done.

"Then look at that Chevy right next to it. It's a '77, but it came from the same assembly line. The body is almost the same."

"Okay ..."

"So that's the example my professor at Tech used to explain it. Cars that look alike. It's how scientists look at fossils too. How they can tell that one life-form comes from the next ... You know, evolution."

Oh. By that time they had followed the crowd off the grandstands and were making their way to Uncle John's minivan out in the parking lot. Who was she to argue with a college kid? And yet ... something occurred to Izzy about what her cousin was trying to tell her. She turned to him after they'd piled into the backseat.

"Those cars you pointed out ..." she started.

"Yup." Alex knew the answers. "Just another illustration of evolution."

"Whatever." This time she couldn't just smile and nod. "I was just wondering, though. Do you think a real person designed the older car?"

"Well, sure." This time Alex's face clouded a bit.

"And did a real person design the newer car too?"

"Sure, but — "

"And would there be a chance the designer might have used some of the same ideas, or maybe some of the same drawings, for both cars?"

Alex frowned and sighed this time.

"That's not the point."

Wasn't it? Izzy tried not to rub it in, just let her cousin stew on it. Yeah, so if the cars looked like they were related, that could mean the same person thought them up. Couldn't it?

Just like in creation. Only in creation it would be the same *God* who used the same kind of plans for the things — and the people — he made.

Good example, Alex, she thought, and she tried to keep from smiling as they drove away from the fairgrounds.

"Thanks for taking us to the derby," she told her uncle John. "Maybe we should do it again next year."

Briefcase

- A scientist named Tim Berra wrote a book called *Evolution and the Myth of Creationism* in 1990. In it, he said that Corvettes can help us understand evolution, because we can see how they changed from year to year. Whoops! Somebody forgot to tell Professor Berra that Corvettes don't have baby Corvettes. And that Corvettes are designed by intelligent people. So Tim Berra scored a goal for the other side, since his argument was really for intelligent design! Today, it's called Berra's Blunder.

- No one is quite sure when the first demolition derbies were held. Some think a stock-car driver named Larry Mendelsohn organized the first one in Long Island, New York, in the late 1950s. But the Merriam-Webster's dictionary first included the term "demolition derby" in their 1953 edition. That means there were probably demolition derbies at county fairs at least back in the late 1940s. Anyway, people have been smashing cars for a long time.

Go Ahead, Stump Me!

- What do you think of Alex's argument that cars could help us understand evolution? What's wrong with his argument?

- According to the Bible (see John 1:1), who or what made God? When was God created?

- Do you think everything has a cause? Why or why not?

- How did Izzy use something ordinary like a demolition derby to explain what she believed? What are some ways you can do the same thing?

Chapter 9
DOUBLE-SPACED

I 'm not saying there couldn't be aliens some-where." Madison looked out through the win-dows of their three-seat lunar landing simulator. The earth, which had looked far off before, now nearly filled their view. "I'm just saying I don't *think* so."

"What?" Travis, the flight commander, sat in the middle seat of three. "You don't think out of all those millions and billions of planets out there, there could be life on at least one? Oh, wait," he said. "I forgot. You still believe in the Sunday school version."

"If you mean that I believe God created all this ..." She meant all the space they could see out their window. The fake stars looked so real. Especially the big blue planet. "Then yeah. A lot of astronauts get up into space and see how God created everything."

The simulator lurched and some lights started flashing. But Travis only chuckled and shook his head.

"Not when they get back down to Earth." He waved his hand at the globe, bigger and closer. They could see the outline of Africa now, and the Atlantic Ocean. "I mean, come on. A little air, a little water, a little heat, a few million years, and there you go. What's so special about this place that it couldn't happen a thousand million times over?"

Madison sighed. Not again. Before they'd come on this field trip to Space Camp, she'd promised herself not to get into any discussions with the class brainiac. As her best friend, Samantha Ortiz, had warned her, nobody out-nerded the Nerd.

"But it's perfect where it is," she tried. "If we

were a few miles farther away from the sun, we'd float away."

"Yeah, wouldn't that be cool?" he joked.

"But if we were a few miles closer," Madison explained, "we'd have too much gravity and we'd be like pancakes smashed to the ground. So I don't think it's chance that put us right where we're supposed to be. God's fingerprints are all over this."

Travis shrugged the same way he always did when she tried to argue with him, like he didn't want to be confused with the facts. Now an alarm went off as well. Madison pointed at the blinking yellow light.

"Uh ... aren't we supposed to be doing something, Travis?" she asked. She was no expert, but it wasn't hard to see.

"Sure. Thrusters off, on my mark. Three-two-one ..." Suddenly Travis snapped commands like a shuttle pilot, which only made Madison sweat even more. Uh-oh. She ran her hands across the huge panel of switches and lights in front of her.

"Uh ... right," she replied. "Thrusters. Hang on a sec."

Over on Travis's left, Samantha let out a giggle.

"Come on, you two," Travis snapped. "This is why girls don't go to space very much."

"Hey, that's not true!" Madison wasn't going

to let that one go. "Lots of women go to space, and they do just as well as the men. Sometimes better."

"Not if they can't find their way around the controls." Travis reached over and flipped a red switch right in front of Madison's face. "There. We just crashed into Siberia because you couldn't find the right switch. Little too much gravity, huh?"

"Leave her alone, Travis." Good for Sam, who finally came to Madison's rescue. "You've been inside this simulator thing a hundred times. This is our first time."

Madison couldn't wait to get out. Her closet back home had more room than the little three-seat fake control cockpit thingie, pretending they were flying to the moon and back.

"All right, you three." The tinny voice of a Space Camp instructor came over the speakers behind their heads. "I think you've done enough damage for one flight."

"Amen." Madison looked up when the over-head hatch opened, raising her hands and taking a deep breath of fresh air.

"So is that all you can come up with?" Travis challenged her again as he unfolded his skinny frame from the simulator capsule. "A little thing like gravity?"

"You mean, what's so special about the earth?" she asked again to stall for time, while she thought of an answer that would make more sense. "There's lots of other things."

The trouble was, she couldn't quite think of any. By then their Space Camp counselors had already steered the group down the hall to another event: the centrifuge.

"Now we're talking," Travis said a few minutes later as they were strapped into a little pod about the size of a sports car.

"It's even smaller inside than the last one." Samantha started breathing kind of funny, and Madison patted her hand so she wouldn't totally freak out.

"We'll look back on this and laugh," Madison whispered to her friend. Right. Saying so might help her believe it herself.

"All right." The staff guy in the navy-blue polo shirt got their attention. "Your pod here is on the end of this thirty-foot arm. We'll shut the hatch over you and start you spinning around, which will make it feel like you're inside a spaceship, taking off."

"C-c-c-ool." Samantha's teeth chattered, and she broke a weak smile.

"How many G's are we going to pull?" asked Travis. The staff guy lifted his eyebrows.

"Sounds like you've done this before."

"Seven times." Travis shrugged. "I did the advanced Space Camp overnighter for my last birthday."

"Good." The staff guy smiled. "Then you can tell your friends there's nothing to worry about. We're only going to try for three G's this time, which is three times the force of gravity you feel when you're standing here on the earth. Got it?"

The girls nodded, but Travis only frowned.

"Is that all?" he asked. "Fighter pilots do more than that."

"Well, you're not a fighter pilot." The staff guy smiled as he tightened the spider's web of straps around each of them. "We don't want you blacking out on us."

"Thanks," Madison whispered as the hatch closed. After a couple of seconds and an "all clear" buzzer, they lurched into action. And at first it wasn't so bad.

"Is that it?" Samantha looked over at them with a little smile. Maybe they would survive this, after all.

Or maybe not. Because a moment later Madison felt her head press back into the padded seat. Yikes! Her eyes grew wide, and she could hardly move.

"Feels like ..." Samantha began, forcing out the words, "a big hand ... pressing my face down."

Madison felt like her cheeks had deflated. Like her eyeballs were going to pop. Like she could hardly look to the side to see if the other two were still alive.

But she did, just in time to see the smile disappear from Travis's face. He gurgled a little, but by this time he looked more like the fish Madison had caught last summer in her grandpa's boat on Lake Peregrine, the way it gasped and its eyes bugged out.

But before Madison could figure out what to do — have mercy! — it was over. Slowly she felt the blood return to her cheeks, and she started to breathe easier. Only things weren't so easy for Travis. Even before they'd stopped all the way, he grabbed for a little paper bag in a rack next to their seats. Like he was going to ...

"He's sick!" announced Samantha. Madison didn't know whether to plug her ears or her nose. And she didn't waste any time jumping out of the pod as soon as the doors opened.

"You'll be all right, dude." The staff member helped Travis out last. Everybody who was still in line for the simulator sort of backed up as he walked by, like he had a disease he could give them.

"Ew," said one girl. "What happened to him?"

Madison helped him out of the building into the fresh air. For once he had nothing to say, which really wasn't a bad thing.

"Yeah," she told him. "You'll be okay. You just got a little too much gravity. And gravity's not such a big deal, now, is it?"

Briefcase

- Crunch time. To escape the gravity of Jupiter, a space-craft would have to travel over 134,000 miles per hour! Compare that to how fast space shuttles have to travel to clear the earth's gravity – seven miles a second, or about 25,000 miles per hour. Get too close to Jupiter, and you're not coming back!

- People are made for gravity. Astronauts in space have a great time floating around without gravity. But weightlessness eventually does bad things to bones and blood. Space experiments on rats in spinning cages (kind of like the centrifuge in our story, only not as dizzying) showed animals that got just a little gravity in space came back much healthier.

- Even before the Internet, people in Bible times had a pretty good idea of who set up the earth and the stars. Check out this psalm, written by King David nearly one thousand years before Jesus was born: "I think about the heavens. I think about what your fingers have created. I think about the moon and stars that you have set in place. What is a human being that you think about him? What is a son of man that you take care of him?" (Psalm 8:3 - 4).

Go Ahead, Stump Me!

- What would happen to everything in a world without gravity? Would you be able to float around? Would you float out to space? What would happen to all our water?

- Why do you think just the right amount of gravity points to a Creator? See Psalm 8:3–4 for a hint.

- What would you tell someone who doesn't think there's anything special about our place in the solar system? What if they think it's all chance and the earth just happens to be where it is?

Chapter 10
MY FAVORITE MAESTRO

"Micromachines? What's that?" Kaela trotted double-time to keep up with Thomas while she checked her watch to see how late they were.

Never mind his micro-whatevers. They had less than five minutes until the biggest band concert of the year, "Christmas by Candlelight." In fact, by now she and Thomas should have been sitting down, tuning their violins. Instead, they were racing down the hall halfway across the school with armloads of new music folders.

Yeah, by now everybody and their dog had probably arrived, cramming into the bleachers on both sides of the Franklin Middle School gym.

And by now Mr. Morris was probably going ballistic, wondering what had happened to them. It didn't matter that Kaela hadn't been able to find the right key for the right cabinet to unlock the right drawer containing the folders.

Just hurry.

"It's for Mrs. Snyder's science class," Thomas finally answered. Like she should know what that meant.

"I think my little brother used to play with micromachines," she told him. "Those and the little Matchbox cars."

"No, no." He laughed. "Not that kind of micromachine."

So Thomas explained his project as they hustled down the hall. He didn't seem to care that they were in huge trouble.

"And so these micromachines are a part of each cell," he went on, "like a little machine, and they're all working together, see?"

She saw. Maybe she got a C in science last semester, but she didn't think she was *that* dim.

"And there's no way they can all work totally together unless someone designed it that way. Like a factory. Not just chance, but God. Get it?"

She got it. Maybe this wasn't rocket science, after all.

"You mean ..." She had a thought. "Sort of like a band?"

Like violins and clarinets, drums and trumpets? All the instruments had to work together, or the song wouldn't click.

Thomas looked over at her like maybe she'd said something smart, for once. The problem was, that meant he wasn't watching where he was going, and he wasn't seeing the classroom door that opened up and smacked him off his feet.

"Thomas, watch — !" Kaela tried to sidestep the pileup, but ... never mind. Both their stacks of folders tumbled to the floor in a huge flutter of paper and sheet music.

She groaned and fell to her knees. This was not good. But speaking of Mrs. Snyder, now their science teacher looked as shocked as they probably did. And she was apologizing all over the place.

"I am so sorry, kids!" She tried to pick up a folder or two, but she only mixed things up worse. "I was just grading some papers and remembered it was time for the Winter Concert. Of course I didn't even see you."

"That's okay." Thomas tried to piece together a page one and a page twenty-four with the right pages in between. The problem was, not all the pages had page numbers. Great, huh?

"We'll get it," Kaela told their teacher. "We're kind of late."

"I'll tell your band teacher it was all my fault." She stuffed another bunch of pages into the folders. Pretty nice of her to act concerned, but that still didn't change how late they were.

"That's it." Thomas was in high gear. He must have finally checked his watch.

Three minutes later Thomas and Kaela finally took their places and quickly tuned their violins while everybody else in the band grabbed their music folders. And when Mrs. Snyder whispered something to Mr. Morris, the air went out of his cheery-red cheeks and he nodded. Maybe running into Mrs. Snyder had turned out to be their Get Out of Jail Free card.

"Hey, what took you guys so long?" Andrew Dibble in the clarinet section wanted to know. "We thought Mr. Morris was going to — "

Mr. Morris didn't give him a chance to finish. With one look he shut down the small talk.

Showtime.

And Kaela knew they needed all the help they could get. Each section needed to play the music a hundred percent. Each *micromachine* had to do their thing just right.

Here goes! She lifted her bow, whispered a little prayer, and launched into their version of Tchaikovsky's "Nutcracker Suite."

It sounded pretty good at first. All their practicing had paid off. Thomas hit a bad note, but nobody noticed.

But then came the page turns. It helped that band music was written so people playing different instruments could turn the page at different times. That way it all blended together.

Not this time. All of a sudden the tuba started playing the bass line from "You're a Mean One, Mr. Grinch." Loud. Then a couple of clarinets started different sections of the "Jingle Bell Medley" and "Santa Claus Is Coming to Town." Huh? The drums added a couple of measures from "The Little Drummer Boy."

Rum-pa-pum-pum.

The whole band melted down in the weirdest jumble of music anyone had ever heard, until Mr. Morris brought it all to a halt with a wild wave of his hands.

And that's when Kaela knew her life was *really* over, except for two things.

One, it wasn't really her fault the pages had gotten mixed up, and that everyone had started playing the wrong notes for a few seconds.

And two, she knew that Thomas now had a really, really good example for his science project. Each instrument was sort of like a micromachine, right? And the music wouldn't sound right unless the conductor kept them on the same page, right? So that's how a real body, made by a Creator, had to work too.

Thomas glanced over at her as if he were reading her mind, and gave her a thumbs-up. Yeah, he was thinking the same thing, all right. Had to be. And if he wasn't, well, she would be sure to tell him.

That is, if they ever survived this concert.

Briefcase

- These days, a full symphonic orchestra is often made up of more than one hundred instruments. That means fifty or so violins, violas, basses, and cellos, plus a harp or two. Add a dozen woodwinds made up of flutes, clarinets, oboes, and bassoons. There are about eleven brass, which includes horns, trumpets, trombones, and a tuba. And don't forget the people who bang on things – percussion! Those include timpani, cymbals, bass drums, bells, and a few other goodies.

- Micromachines are one more sign that a Creator made the human body. They're part of each human cell, little tiny work groups that join together to do their thing. And different groups of micromachines do different jobs inside each cell, like rounding up energy to live (sort of like eating) and bringing in fresh air (like breathing). Each job depends on the other, and they all have to be working at the same time. That's about as far from random as you can get!

- You can't see micromachines, but hey, that's why they're called "micro." So where are they? Lots of places, besides in the human cell. Micromachines in cars tell when you're stopping too quickly, and give a signal to blow out the air bags. Also, all cell phones need tiny micromachines (switches, really) to help you talk to your friends. And third, your computer printer head is a micromachine too. That's the part with microscopic, teeny-tiny holes that spits out ink to form letters and shapes.

Go Ahead, Stump Me!

· Whether in a cell or in a larger machine made by a person, how does a micromachine get started? How does it get put together? How do micromachines figure out how to work together?

· To what did Kaela finally compare her band? Why was that a big deal for her to figure out?

· The Bible (1 Corinthians 12:12) says Christians are all part of one body. In a way, does that make us micromachines?

· Have you seen God at work aside from scientific things? Have you ever seen a miracle or something else that can't be explained through science?

Case for Christ for Kids, Updated and Expanded

Lee Strobel

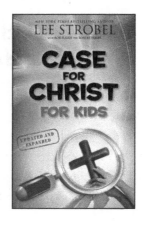

You meet skeptics every day. They ask questions like:

Was Jesus really born in a stable?

Did his friends tell the truth?

Did he really come back from the dead?

Here's a book written in kid-friendly language that gives you all the answers.

Packed full of well-researched, reliable, and eye-opening investigations of some of the biggest questions you have, *Case for Christ for Kids* brings Christ to life by addressing the existence, miracles, ministry, and resurrection of Jesus of Nazareth.

Pick up a copy at your favorite bookstore or online!